Published by Hachette Partworks Ltd
ISBN: 978-1-906965-15-0
Date of Printing: April 2011
Printed in Singapore by Tien Wah Press

Disney Princess

MULAN

Disney

Hachette

Long, long ago, the Emperor of China ordered
that a great wall be built to protect his empire from
China's enemies, the Huns.

In those days in China, a son brought honour to
his family by being a brave soldier. A daughter's
duty was to marry well and be a good wife.

When a girl was the right age for marriage, she would visit the local Matchmaker, who would find her a husband. The visit to the matchmaker was a nerve-wracking ordeal for many girls.

One morning, a girl named Mulan was getting ready for her visit to the local Matchmaker. Mulan was nervous. She was not like other girls: she certainly looked respectable, but would she be able to behave like a perfect wife for her husband?

Mulan's mother put a fine comb in her hair. "There!" she said "you're finally ready!"

"Just one last thing," said her grandmother. "You need something lucky."

She tied a tiny cage to Mulan's belt.

"A cricket will bring you good fortune!" she said.

But when they got to the Matchmaker's, things went badly wrong: poor Mulan was very nervous and the cricket escaped from the cage and hopped onto the Matchmaker's dress, making her shriek.

The frightened woman backed into the stove and her dress caught fire.

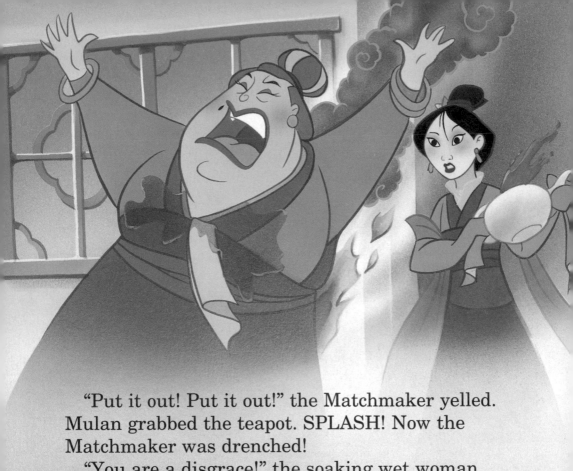

"Put it out! Put it out!" the Matchmaker yelled. Mulan grabbed the teapot. SPLASH! Now the Matchmaker was drenched!

"You are a disgrace!" the soaking wet woman shouted. "You may look like a bride, but you'll never bring your family honour."

Mulan returned home. When Fa Zhou saw
his daughter's face, he guessed things had not
gone well. While she took care of her horse
Khan, Mulan wondered if she could ever
bring honour to the family.

Mulan's father tried to cheer her up.

"What lovely blossoms we have this year," he said. He pointed to an unopened flower on a nearby tree. "Look! This one is late, but I'll bet that when it blooms, it will be the most beautiful of all."

Mulan smiled. Her father was saying that one day she would bring honour to her family.

Just as Mulan
was starting
to feel better,
she heard the
beating of a
drum.

Mulan climbed
the wall and saw
the Emperor's
advisor, Chi Fu.

"The Huns have
invaded China!" Chi Fu
announced.

"By order of the Emperor, one man
from every family must serve in the Imperial
Army!"

Fa Zu had been a great warrior in his
younger days, but time had passed and an old
wound had weakened him. Mulan's heart sank
when she saw him in his army uniform: she
realised that he would never survive a battle.
She devised a plan to save his life.

As soon as night fell, Mulan silently crept into her parents' bedroom, took the imperial scroll summoning her father and replaced it with her comb as a mark of devotion.

Then she took the sword and, with one swipe, she cut off her long black hair.

Mulan put on her father's army uniform and
left the house. She looked like any young soldier
going to war – and this was her plan. She would
pretend to be a boy and take her father's place in
the army.

As the cold rain fell, Mulan mounted her
faithful horse Khan. She rode off, not knowing if
she would ever see her family again.

Later that night, Mulan's parents discovered what she had done. They were shocked. Impersonating a soldier was a crime and if Mulan was caught, she would be put to death. But there was nothing they could do.

Mulan's grandmother prayed for help. "Ancestors, hear our prayer," she pleaded. "Watch over Mulan."

In the family temple, the Ancestors of the Fa family listened to the old woman's prayer and decided to send a guardian to protect Mulan.

A small dragon called Mushu volunteered for the task but the Ancestors made fun of him. Mushu wasn't deemed worthy of the role of Family Guardian.

The Ancestors didn't think Mushu could do the job, so they ordered him to use his gong and awaken the most powerful Guardian of all – the Great Stone Dragon.

Mushu approached the old statue. "Yo, Rocky!" he called. "Wake up!"

But the Great Stone Dragon did not wake up. So Mushu climbed up the statue and loudly banged the gong right against its ear!

"Hello! Hellooo!" he yelled. Suddenly, the dragon's ear broke off. "Uh-oh," said Mushu.

Then the whole statue began to crack, and it crumbled to pieces!

"Oh man, they're gonna kill me!" said the terrified dragon.

Just then, Mushu spotted Cri-Kee, Mulan's lucky cricket, and had an idea: if he could turn Mulan into a hero, the Ancestors would forgive him and let him be Guardian again.

Cri-Kee and Mushu caught up with Mulan, but the dragon was afraid that the girl wouldn't take him seriously. So he cast an enormous shadow onto a rock face to fool her into thinking that he was a very large, powerful and wise dragon!

When Mulan saw the tiny Mushu come out from behind the rock, she was astonished. "Who are you?" she asked.

"I am the powerful, indestructible Mushu at your service!" was the reply.

Mulan wasn't convinced, but she allowed the little dragon to accompany her. She needed all the help she could get!

Later, Mulan reached the Imperial Army camp, where she met three soldiers, Yao, Ling and Chien-Po. Trying to act like a man, she greeted Yao by punching him in the shoulder.

But her gesture, instead of cementing a friendship, led to a big fight! Luckily, Captain Shang's voice succeeded in restoring order: "Soldiers! Save your strength for tomorrow. You'll need it!"

The next day, the men began their training. Shang shot an arrow into the top of a very high pole and ordered Yao to go and retrieve it. But first, he tied two heavy bronze discs to Yao's wrists. "One of these discs represents strength," he explained. "The other, discipline. You're going to need both…"

But Yao could not manage to climb to the top of the pole – no one could. During the days that followed, the recruits doubled their efforts, but nobody succeeded.

Shang's challenge was tough for Mulan, but just when she was about to give up, she had a brilliant idea. She tied the two discs together, and she used their weight to help her climb to the top of the pole.

The soldiers gave her a round of applause and even Shang smiled!

Finally, when all the men were fit for battle, the army mobilised.

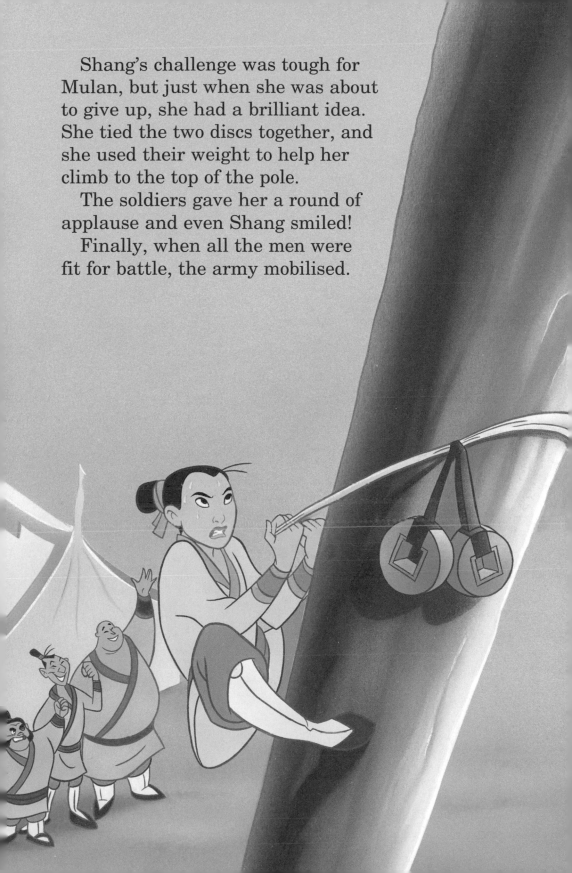

A few days later, while they were marching, a
shower of arrows began to rain down on them.
   It was the Huns, led by Shan-Yu, their
ruthless leader!

Immediately, Shang gave the order for the cannons to fire: "BOOM! BOOM!"

Despite Shang's efforts, the Huns were winning.
"Aim at Shan-Yu!" shouted Shang in desperation.
But Mulan had an idea. She took the last of the
ammunition but, instead of aiming it at Shan-Yu,
she aimed at the snowy slopes above him.

WHUMP! The cannonball exploded into the mountain, making the ground tremble and causing the snow to start moving. Mulan's plan had worked: the tremors from the explosion had set off an avalanche!

Shan-Yu, realising what was happening, attacked Mulan, but it was too late: the snow was already overwhelming the Huns.

Mulan had become a hero. She had disobeyed Shang's command, but she had saved the Army and beaten the Huns.

"You are the craziest man I know!" said Shang. "But I owe you my life. Because of this, you have gained my trust."

Mulan suddenly felt faint: she had been wounded by Shan-Yu in the battle and she collapsed to the ground.

She was taken to the hospital where the doctor found out the truth: this soldier was a woman!

Shang could not believe it. "I did it to save my father's life," the girl explained. Shang didn't reply. Even though Mulan had acted bravely, she had committed a crime and had to be punished.

Shang raised his sword, but he couldn't bring
himself to hurt the girl who had saved his life.
He lowered his weapon.

"A life for a life!" he declared. Then he set off
with his army, leaving Mulan and Khan behind on
the frozen mountain.

Mulan felt despair: she had failed and dishonoured her father. Mushu did his best to cheer her up.

"Come on," he said. "Don't worry. You risked your life for your loved ones. Your intentions were good."

Just then, Mushu spotted Shan-Yu and five of his men, heading towards the Imperial City.

"We have to do something!" Mulan cried. She jumped up, grabbed her sword, and raced towards Khan.

Mushu hesitated. "Are we in this together or not?" Mulan asked the little dragon.

"Yeah!" Mushu agreed. "Let's go kick some Hunny buns!" With Cri-Kee safely on board, they all rode off to the Imperial City.

Mulan arrived in the Imperial City to find Shang and his men in a parade to celebrate the defeat of the Huns.

"Shang!" Mulan cried. "The Huns are alive!" They're in the city!"

"Why should I believe you?" Shang replied coldly. Shang ignored Mulan. He rode off to the Imperial Palace to meet the Emperor.

As soon as the parade reached the Emperor's palace, one of the dragons in the parade split apart: the Huns had hidden in it to get inside the palace! They knocked Shang unconscious, kidnapped the Emperor and locked him inside his palace.

They had to rescue the Emperor, but how?

Then Mulan had another idea: she dressed as a woman, and Yao, Ling and Chien-Po did the same. They climbed the Palace's walls and approached Shan-Yu's men. They were delighted to see the four women!

The foursome soon overpowered the Huns, but
Shan-Yu was still holding the Emperor captive.
"Bow to me!" he ordered. But the Emperor
refused – he bowed to no-one!

Luckily, just at that moment Shang rushed in and managed to disarm Shan-Yu.

Meanwhile, Chien-Po carried the Emperor to safety.

Shan-Yu gave Shang the slip and set off across the
rooftops to find Mulan. But she was ready for him.
"Ready, Mushu?" cried Mulan. "Yes!" replied
Mushu, launching a rocket towards Shan-Yu. The
evil Hun was finished!

As a thank-you, the Emperor presented Mulan
with his own pendant and Shan-Yu's sword.

"When they see this pendant, your family will
know you saved the Emperor's life. And when they
see this sword, they'll know you saved China!"

Then the Emperor did the unthinkable: he bowed
to Mulan as a mark of respect!

Mulan returned home. Her mother and grandmother wept with joy and her father was filled with pride.

Before long, Mulan had a surprise visitor. It was Shang. Mulan asked him to stay for dinner, and Shang happily accepted. Mulan's family watched the two with quiet contentment. They sensed a very special relationship was blooming.

As for Mushu, when the Ancestors learned of his deeds, they no longer laughed at the little dragon. They celebrated, and Mushu became an official Guardian again. Mushu was thrilled. "Send out for egg rolls!" he cried.